Inside the NBA

# Atlanta Hawks

Bob Italia



ABDO & Daughters
PUBLISHING

Published by Abdo & Daughters, 4940 Viking Dr., Suite 622, Edina, MN 55435.



Cover photo: Wide World Photos
Interior photos: Allsport, pages 1, 5, 20, 23, 24, 27
Wide World Photos, pages 8, 12, 15, 17

**Edited by Ken Berg**

**Library of Congress Cataloging–in–Publication Data**

Italia, Bob, 1955-
The Atlanta Hawks / Bob Italia
p. cm. — (Inside the NBA)
Includes index.
Summary: Provides an overview of the history and key personalities connected with the team that began play in the new NBA as the Tri-City Blackhawks in the 1049-50 season.
ISBN 1-56239-750-8
1. Atlanta Hawks (Basketball team)—Juvenile literature. [1. Atlanta Hawks (Basketball team)—History. 2. Basketball—History.] I. Title. II. Series.
GV885.52. A7I83 1997
796.323' 64758' 231—dc21 96-39613
CIP
AC

# Contents

# Atlanta Hawks

When the subject is tradition, the Atlanta Hawks aren't the first National Basketball Association (NBA) team that comes to mind. But the team's history began in 1946, when the squad was known as the Tri-Cities Blackhawks. The team then was shared by the cities of Moline and Rock Island, Illinois, and Davenport, Iowa. In later years, the team belonged to Milwaukee and then St. Louis, and enjoyed the services of a handful of the NBA's most memorable stars. In 1958, as the St. Louis Hawks, the club earned the franchise's only championship.

For the 1968-69 season, the franchise moved to Atlanta, where they have been ever since. In Atlanta, the Hawks have usually stayed in the middle of the pack, advancing to the playoffs only to be ousted in the early rounds. Today, however, the team is breaking away from the middle of the pack. Led by their All-Stars, center Dikembe Mutombo and forward Christian Laettner, the Hawks are looking to get that elusive second championship.

*Facing page:* The Hawks' Dikembe Mutombo.

55
MIA

# Early Years

The Tri-Cities Blackhawks joined the National Basketball League (NBL) in 1946-47, when the NBL included the Toledo Jeeps, Youngstown Bears, Oshkosh All-Stars, and Sheboygan Redskins. Tri-Cities finished out of the playoffs in 1946-47, but improved its record to .500 the following year and made it to the first round of the postseason.

At the start of the 1948-49 season, George Mikan's Minneapolis Lakers and three other NBL teams jumped to the Basketball Association of America (BAA). The 1948-49 Blackhawks featured Don Otten, the NBL's only remaining 7-footer. He led the league in scoring with 14 points per game and powered Tri-Cities into the playoffs with a 36-28 record. The Blackhawks survived the first round, but lost to the Oshkosh All-Stars in the second.

After three years of battling, the NBL and the BAA joined forces in 1949-50. Only half of the NBL's 10 franchises survived the merger. Tri-Cities was 1 of the 17 teams in the newly named National Basketball Association (NBA).

In their first NBA contest, the Blackhawks faced the Denver Nuggets and won 93-85. But after six straight losses, Head Coach Roger Potter was fired and Arnold "Red" Auerbach was hired in his place.

Auerbach posted a 28-29 record—good enough to reach the playoffs. But the Blackhawks lost in the first round to the Anderson Packers. Next season, Auerbach moved on to the Boston Celtics.

At the start of the 1950-51 season, the NBA had 11 teams remaining. The Blackhawks went through three coaches that year—Dave McMillan, John Logan, and Mike Todorovich—and finished in last place in the Western Division with a 25-43 record.

Before the start of the 1951-52 season, owner Ben Kerner transferred the club from Tri-Cities to Milwaukee, where a new 10,000-seat arena was waiting. The team—now called the Milwaukee Hawks—played average basketball. The team finished dead last in the Western Division with a 17-49 record.

The 1952-53 Hawks fared better, winning 27 games, but they were stil! the worst team in the Western Division and finished out of the playoffs once again.

With 26 games left on the schedule, Kerner brought in William "Red" Holzman as the new coach. During the offseason, the Hawks added the cornerstone of their future success by drafting 6-foot, 9-inch Louisiana State forward Bob Pettit. He had a spectacular rookie season in 1954-55, averaging 20.4 points (fourth in the NBA) and winning NBA Rookie of the Year honors. Milwaukee improved that season, but remained the weakest in the West at 26-46.

Milwaukee sports fans had by then shifted affections from basketball's Hawks to baseball's Braves. So owner Ben Kerner moved the club to St. Louis, where they were a hit. Pettit was already well on his way to stardom, winning the 1955-56 NBA Most Valuable Player (MVP) Award after leading the league in both scoring (25.7 ppg) and rebounding (16.2 rpg).

Halfway through the season, Kerner improved Pettit's supporting cast with the addition of 6-foot, 7-inch Jack Coleman and 6-foot, 1-inch Jack McMahon. After occupying the bottom rung of the Western Division the previous four seasons, St. Louis climbed to a tie for second place with the Minneapolis Lakers at 33-39. The Lakers beat the Hawks in a one-game playoff and were officially awarded second place.

The two teams met in a best-of-three playoff series, and the Hawks prevailed to move on to the Western Division Finals. They pounced on the Fort Wayne Pistons in the first two games of the five-game series, but Fort Wayne bounced back to sweep the next three.

# A Playoff Shocker

St. Louis got off to a slow start in 1956-57. With the club at 14-19, Red Holzman was fired and Slater Martin took over as player-coach. The team went 5-3 under Martin, but he decided he'd rather remain a player, so reserve forward Alex Hannum was given the reins.

Led by Pettit, the Hawks shared first place in the Western Division with the Minneapolis Lakers and the Fort Wayne Pistons. The three teams finished 34-38.

St. Louis beat Fort Wayne and Minneapolis in single-game playoffs to determine the division champion. St. Louis then swept the Lakers in the Western Division Finals, earning the right to face Boston in the NBA Finals. The Finals were expected to be a Boston romp. But the Hawks pushed them to seven games before losing.

Bob Pettit goes airborne to sink a two-pointer.

# A Finals Rematch

Under Coach Alex Hannum, the 1957-58 Hawks cruised to the top of the Western Division. A rematch of the previous season's climactic Finals took shape after the Hawks eliminated the Pistons, four games to one, and the Celtics took out the Philadelphia Warriors in similar fashion.

This time no one was predicting an easy go of it for Boston. In Game 6, Pettit set a new NBA playoff record by scoring 50 points. The Hawks won by a single point, 110-109, to dethrone the Celtics and claim the crown. Despite winning the title, owner Ben Kerner opted to change coaches for the 1958-59 campaign.

Andy Phillip lasted only 10 games before Ed Macauley took over. The tough veteran team ran away with the Western Division. Pettit earned his second NBA MVP Award after leading the league with 29.2 points per game and setting a new NBA record with 2,105 total points for the season.

The Hawks, who finished with a 49-23 record, were anticipating a third straight Finals matchup with the Celtics. But St. Louis was shocked in the Western Division Finals when Minneapolis, led by rookie Elgin Baylor, took the series, four games to two.

# Back To The Finals

In 1959-60, the Hawks ran away with the Western Division crown for the third consecutive season. St. Louis beat Minneapolis in a seven-game Western Division Finals, while the Celtics rolled over Philadelphia. But 1960 was not a repeat of 1957 as Boston came away with a Game 7 victory.

Owner Ben Kerner changed coaches again during the offseason, replacing Ed Macauley with Paul Seymour. The only other significant change was the addition of rookie Lenny Wilkens. The 6-foot, 1-inch guard averaged 11.7 points in his first year as St. Louis took the Western Division title by a 15-game margin.

Los Angeles pushed St. Louis to seven games in the Western Division Finals, but the Hawks made it to the championship round. Unfortunately, Boston made short work of the weary Hawks.

The following season was disastrous for St. Louis as Wilkens was called to military duty. Kerner shuffled through three coaches, first firing Seymour after 14 games. His replacement, Andrew "Fuzzy" Levane, lasted 60 contests. Pettit was tapped to lead the club for the season's final six games. The Hawks finished with a dismal 29-51 record and fell to fourth place in the Western Division, ending a five-year reign at the top. The club also finished out of the playoffs for the first time in six seasons.

# Housecleaning

After the disastrous 1961-62 season, Kerner did some major housecleaning as he brought in Harry "the Horse" Gallatin as head coach. Gallatin kept Pettit and Hagan. After a one-year absence, Wilkens was back from the army. Another key acquisition was draft pick Zelmo Beaty.

The changes paid off. In 1962-63, St. Louis rebounded to a 48-32 mark and finished second in the West behind the Los Angeles Lakers. Pettit continued his scoring and rebounding onslaught with 28.4 points and 15.1 rebounds per game. Beaty was named to the NBA All-Rookie Team after averaging 10.2 points and 8.3 rebounds, and Gallatin won the first-ever NBA Coach of the Year Award. The Hawks eliminated Detroit in the Western Division Semifinals, then pushed the Lakers to seven games in the Western Division Finals before bowing out.

Two games into the 1963-64 campaign, the Hawks signed veteran guard Richie Guerin from the Knicks. St. Louis finished second in the West again, this time trailing the San Francisco Warriors by two games. The Hawks got by Los Angeles in the opening round of postseason play but were ousted by the Warriors in a seven-game Western Division Finals.

The Hawks got off to a poor start the following year. Pettit missed 30 games with a knee injury, and Guerin was sidelined with a leg problem. After the team got off to a slow start, Kerner fired Gallatin and replaced him with Guerin, who became player-coach. The team went 28-19 under Guerin to secure second place in the Western Division. But the Hawks were upset in the first round of the playoffs by the Baltimore Bullets, three games to one.

Zelmo Beaty battles for the ball against a heavy Cincinnati defense.

# Pettit Calls It Quits

Pettit retired after the 1964-65 season. He completed his 11-year career with averages of 26.4 points and 16.2 rebounds per game. He was an All-NBA First Team selection 10 times, the All-Star Game MVP four times, and NBA MVP twice. He was also the first NBA player to score 20,000 points.

The team struggled in the 1965-66 season with Pettit gone. Zelmo Beaty averaged 20.7 points and 13.6 rebounds. St. Louis finished in third place behind Baltimore, then avenged the previous season's playoff upset with a three-game sweep of the Bullets. The Hawks then surprised everyone by taking the Lakers to seven games in the Western Division Finals before bowing out.

# "Sweet Lou" Makes His Debut

The Hawks selected 6-foot, 5-inch shooter Lou Hudson in the 1966 NBA Draft. Hudson had a dazzling rookie season, leading the club with an average of 18.4 points per game. He was named to the NBA All-Rookie Team at season's end. St. Louis took second place in the Western Division despite finishing three games under .500.

In the playoffs, the Hawks swept the expansion Chicago Bulls before bowing to the San Francisco Warriors in the Western Division Finals, four games to two.

The 1967-68 Hawks breezed through the Western Division, taking the crown with a 56-26 record. However, the third-place Warriors surprised the Hawks in the playoffs by taking a first-round series in six games. On May 3, 1968, owner Ben Kerner announced that the Hawks had been sold to Georgia real estate developer Thomas Cousins and former Georgia Governor Carl Sanders.

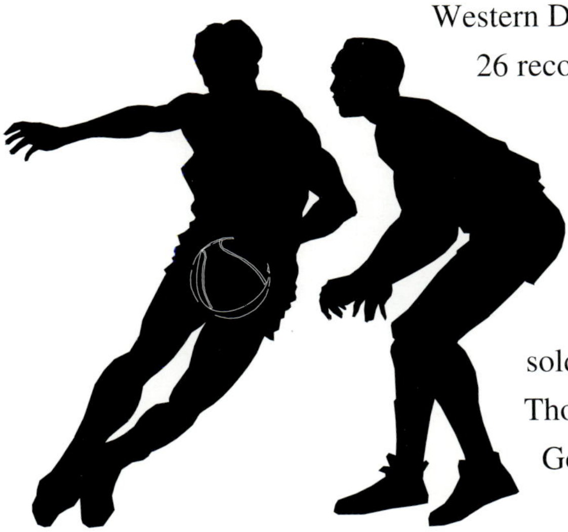

# Hawks Fly South

The new owners moved the franchise to Atlanta and retained Guerin as coach. A contract dispute forced management to trade Lenny Wilkens to Seattle for Walt Hazzard.

In 1968-69, Atlanta finished seven games behind the Western Division-champion Los Angeles Lakers, then fell to the Lakers in the Western Division Finals, winning only one game.

The Hawks were Western Division champions in 1969-70, but they had to do it without Zelmo Beaty, who had jumped to the American Basketball Association (ABA). The late-season addition of Detroit's Walt Bellamy helped fill the void. Atlanta made short work of the Chicago Bulls in the first round of the 1970 NBA playoffs, then ran into Wilt Chamberlain and Elgin Baylor in the Western Division Finals. The Lakers dismantled the Hawks in four straight.

Joe Caldwell defected to the ABA prior to the 1970-71 season. The addition of rookie scoring sensation Pete Maravich proved to be a mixed blessing. Although Maravich finished second on the team in scoring with 23.2 points per game (behind Lou Hudson's 26.8 ppg), the team often didn't know what to make of his fancy passing and showboat dribbling. For the first time since moving to Atlanta, the Hawks fell below .500, finishing at 36-46. They were no match for the New York Knicks in the playoffs and fell in five games.

The 1971-72 season was a repeat performance. The Hawks finished 10 games below the .500 mark and were booted in the first round of the playoffs, falling to Boston in six games.

# A New Arena And Coach

During the offseason, the Hawks moved into the new 16,500-seat Omni. The club also experienced the end of the Richie Guerin era. After 7½ seasons at the helm, Guerin stepped aside, leaving with a 327-291 career record. To replace Guerin, the Hawks hired Lowell "Cotton" Fitzsimmons, who arrived in Atlanta from the Phoenix Suns.

Propelled by the high-scoring duo of Hudson (27.1 ppg) and Maravich (26.1), the Hawks finished at 46-36. But for the second year in a row, Atlanta fell victim to Boston in the first round of the playoffs.

During the 1973-74 season, Maravich finished No. 2 in the league in scoring with 27.7 points per game. But the team finished 35-47 and out of the playoffs, ending an 11-year run of postseason appearances.

Pete Maravich passes off the ball.

# "Pistol Pete" Says Good-Bye

The Hawks unloaded Maravich in the offseason, sending him to the expansion New Orleans Jazz for Dean Meminger and Bob Kauffman. During the 1974-75 season, Atlanta won only 31 times, the team's lowest victory total since 1961-62.

The Hawks held together for the first three months of the 1975-76 campaign and reached February 1 with a 23-25 record. The emergence of second-year forward John Drew, who scored 21.6 points per game, helped. But the team collapsed during the second half, winning only 6 of its final 34 games. Fitzsimmons was released with eight games left in the season.

Hubie Brown took over for 1976-77. But Brown couldn't do much for the undermanned Hawks in his first season, and the team finished out of the playoffs for the fourth year in a row, at 31-51.

Wayne "Tree" Rollins maneuvers around a tight Buffalo Braves defense.

# Turner Takes Over

In January, Ted Turner (who owned the Atlanta Braves and an Atlanta television station) announced that he had purchased the NBA franchise. Atlanta traded Hudson at the end of the 1976-77 season, to the Los Angeles Lakers for Ollie Johnson.

In the 1977 NBA Draft, the Hawks picked up 7-foot, 1-inch center Wayne "Tree" Rollins and 6-foot, 2-inch guard Eddie Johnson. Coach Brown somehow managed to coax 10 more wins out of his young squad, and the 1977-78 Hawks finished with a 41-41 record, earning the team a spot in the playoffs and Brown the NBA Coach of the Year Award.

Atlanta continued its progress under Coach Brown. Dan Roundfield joined the team for the 1978-79 campaign. The Hawks improved to 46-36 and took third place in the Central Division, only two games behind the first-place San Antonio Spurs.

In the playoffs, Atlanta dismantled the Houston Rockets in a best-of-three first-round series, then stretched Washington to the limit in the Eastern Conference Semifinals before losing in Game 7.

# Atlanta

Bob Pettit, drafted by the Hawks in 1954, was the first NBA player to score over 20,000 points.

Zelmo Beaty was named to the NBA All-Rookie Team for the 1962-63 season.

For the 1973-74 season, Pete Maravich finished second in the league in scoring with 27.7 points per game.

# Hawks

In 11 seasons with Atlanta, Dominique Wilkins scored 23,292 points.

Christian Laettner was named an Eastern Conference All-Star for the 1996-97 season.

Eastern Conference All-Star Dikembe Mutombo led the Hawks to the playoffs in the 1996-97 season.

Dominique Wilkins sets up for a free throw.

# Hawks Soar To The Title

The Hubie Brown-era Hawks came into their own in 1979-80. A well-balanced team led by Drew, Roundfield, Rollins, and Johnson won 50 games and came out on top in the Central Division. It was the Hawks' first division title since 1970, and the first 50-win season for the franchise since 1967-68.

Unfortunately, the solid regular-season play did not carry over into the playoffs. An inspired Philadelphia 76ers led by Julius Erving made short work of the Hawks in the Eastern Conference Semifinals, winning the series four games to one.

Inexplicably, the 1980-81 Hawks collapsed. The team finished 20 games under .500 and plummeted from first to fourth place in the Central Division. And Brown's tenure ended after five seasons.

Turner brought in Kevin Loughery as the new coach for the 1981-82 season. Loughery took the same crew and turned it into a tight defensive unit. The team led the league in defense in 1981-82, holding opponents to only 100.5 points per contest. The Hawks improved to a 42-40 mark and made the playoffs, losing a first-round series to Philadelphia.

On September 3, 1982, the Hawks sent John Drew and Freeman Williams to the Utah Jazz for rookie Dominique Wilkins. The former University of Georgia star earned a spot on the 1982-83 NBA All-Rookie Team by averaging 17.5 points. Rollins led the league in blocked shots with 343. Roundfield led the team in scoring (19.0 ppg) and rebounding (11.4 rpg). But the Hawks won only one game more than in the previous season and were once again eliminated from postseason play in the first round.

Mike Fratello replaced Loughery before the 1983-84 campaign. In his first year, the club fell to two games below .500 but made it to the playoffs. For 1984-85, the Hawks embarked on a major rebuilding program. Roundfield was dealt to the Pistons for 6-foot, 8-inch Cliff Levingston, 6-foot, 9-inch Antoine Carr, and a couple of draft picks.

Atlanta also picked up 7-footer Kevin Willis in the 1984 NBA Draft. Wilkins finished sixth in the league in scoring with 27.4 points per game, and the Hawks finished fifth in the Central Division with a 34-48 record. In the offseason, Atlanta drafted Jon Koncak and then signed Anthony "Spud" Webb to a free-agent deal.

The Hawks were the second-youngest team in the NBA heading into the 1985-86 season, and expectations were low. After a slow start, the team eventually nailed down a 50-win season. Wilkins led the league in scoring with 30.3 points per game and made his first All-Star appearance. Fratello was named NBA Coach of the Year.

But the most impressive feat was performed by the 5-foot, 7-inch Webb, who thrilled fans and teammates alike by winning the NBA Slam-Dunk Championship on NBA All-Star Saturday.

After a one-year absence, the Hawks returned to the playoffs in 1986. They got by the Pistons in the first round, thanks to a double-overtime win in Game 4. But Atlanta was no match for the Celtics in the Eastern Conference Semifinals. Boston dispatched the Hawks in five games, routing the young team by 33 points in Game 5.

# A Two-Year Run For The NBA Title

One year later, the Hawks joined the league's elite. The team cruised to a Central Division title with a franchise-record 57 wins. The club was led by Dominique Wilkins, who finished second in the league to Michael Jordan in scoring with 29 points per game.

With high expectations, the Hawks soared into the postseason and eliminated the Indiana Pacers, three games to one, in the opening round. But Atlanta fell in five games to the Pistons in the Eastern Conference Semifinals.

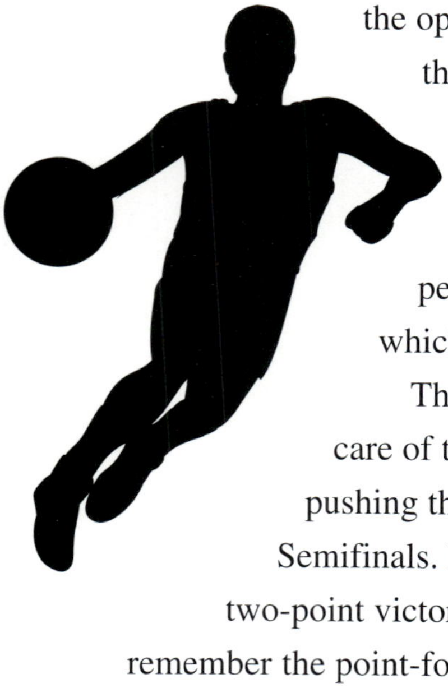

The Hawks failed to repeat as Central Division champs in 1987-88, but managed to win 50 games behind Wilkins's 30.7 points per game. It marked the third straight season in which Atlanta had claimed at least 50 wins.

They made a strong run in the playoffs, taking care of the Milwaukee Bucks in five games and then pushing the Celtics to the limit in the Eastern Conference Semifinals. In a hard-fought series, Boston prevailed with two-point victories in Games 6 and 7. NBA fans will long remember the point-for-point, basket-for-basket duel between Wilkins and Larry Bird in the fourth quarter of Game 7.

# Injuries Hurt Hawks

The Hawks made some monumental deals prior to the 1988-89 campaign. On June 27, they picked up Reggie Theus from the Sacramento Kings. Six weeks later, Atlanta signed 13-year veteran Moses Malone to a free-agent contract. The team seemed to be ready to challenge for a title, but before the season opened, Kevin Willis fractured his left foot and was lost for the year.

Even without Willis, the Hawks turned in another 50-win performance. But the club was stunned by the Milwaukee Bucks in the first round of the playoffs.

Atlanta's run of 50-win seasons ended at four when the Hawks fell to 41-41 in 1989-90, as injuries wiped out the backcourt and the bench. Their record was not good enough to make the playoffs.

*Right:* Moses Malone drives hard to the hoop.

BONUS
QUARTER
Hawks
21
Orlando
31
Hawks
42

# Changing Of The Guard

Mike Fratello lost his coaching job because of his team's mediocre showing. He left the franchise with the second best coaching record with 324 victories, only 3 fewer than Richie Guerin. Atlanta courted former San Antonio Head Coach Bob Weiss and named him the new boss on May 22, 1990.

In the 1990-91 season, Atlanta finished with a 43-39 record. Back in the playoffs after a one-year absence, the Hawks fell to the Pistons in a five-game first-round series.

During the offseason, the team sent guard Doc Rivers to the Los Angeles Clippers. Atlanta used their first-round pick to obtain Stacey Augmon, a 6-foot, 8-inch swingman and defensive specialist from the University of Nevada-Las Vegas. The Hawks also dealt Spud Webb to the Sacramento Kings and then turned the point guard position over to second-year player Rumeal Robinson. Despite their young backcourt, the Hawks finished the 1991-92 season with a 38-44 record.

In 1992-93, Wilkins scored 31 points against the Seattle SuperSonics in February to pass Bob Pettit as the all-time leading scorer in franchise history. The team entered the playoffs as the No. 7 seed in the Eastern Conference. That meant a first-round appointment with the Chicago Bulls. The three-game series was a rout. A 10-point loss in Game 3 was the closest Atlanta could get to Chicago, which swept the series.

*Facing page:* Dominique Wilkins slams one in for two points.

# Division Title

Lenny Wilkens, who replaced Bob Weiss as head coach for the 1993-94 season, brought defense, winning, and excitement to Atlanta. The team went 57-25, tying the franchise record for victories in a season and capturing its first Central Division title since 1987. Although the Hawks were upset by the Indiana Pacers in the Eastern Conference Semifinals, Wilkens was named NBA Coach of the Year. By season's end, his 926 career coaching victories left him only 12 short of Red Auerbach's 938 for the top spot on the NBA's all-time list.

The Hawks changed their lineup significantly in February, trading their all-time scoring leader, Dominique Wilkins, to the Los Angeles Clippers for Danny Manning. Wilkins left Atlanta having accumulated 23,292 points in 11 seasons.

After needing five games to eliminate the Miami Heat in the first round, the Hawks were upended by the Pacers, who had won 10 fewer games than Atlanta during the regular season.

Danny Manning didn't stay with Atlanta for long, opting to accept a free-agency deal with the Phoenix Suns instead. The Hawks then made a significant trade as the 1994-95 season opened, sending Kevin Willis and a future draft pick to the Miami Heat for Steve Smith, Grant Long, and a future second-round draft selection. The Hawks finished at 42-40 and were dispatched from the playoffs by the Indiana Pacers in three games.

The big story for Atlanta in 1994-95 was Head Coach Lenny Wilkens, who became the NBA's all-time leader in coaching victories. In his 22nd season as an NBA coach, Wilkens passed Red Auerbach's 938 wins when the Hawks defeated the Washington Bullets on January 6.

Christian Laettner drives the ball toward the basket.

# The 1995-96 Season

During the 1995-96 season, the Hawks acquired an all-around solid player in Christian Laettner, along with Sean Rooks, in a trade with the Minnesota Timberwolves for Andrew Lang and Spud Webb. Laettner averaged 14.2 points and 7.8 rebounds with Atlanta. Wilkens became the first NBA coach to win 1,000 games with a victory over Cleveland on March 1 at the Omni. Wilkens' total was boosted to 1,014 by the end of the season as the Hawks finished with a 46-36 record and the No. 6 position in the Eastern Conference playoffs.

The Hawks defeated the Pacers 3-2, in the first round, winning the decisive fifth game in Indiana. Atlanta was then eliminated in the Eastern Conference Semifinals, 4-1, by the powerful Orlando Magic, but the Hawks did avoid being swept by winning Game 4 in Atlanta.

# A Bright Future

Before the 1996-97 season began, Atlanta acquired free-agent center Dikembe Mutombo. This forced the Hawks to trade two starters: forward Grant Long, and guard/forward Stacey Augmon. But in the end the signing of Mutombo radically improved the Hawks. Laettner was helped by the trade, moving to power-forward. Mutombo and Laettner became a real force in the NBA. Both players were Eastern Conference All-Stars.

The Hawks played consistent basketball throughout the 1996-97 season. Led by Mutombo and Laettner, Atlanta won 56 games. In the first round of the playoffs they met the talented Detroit Pistons. In a hard fought series the Hawks won in five grueling games.

In the next round, Atlanta was matched against the defending NBA champs, the Chicago Bulls. The Hawks played solid ball throughout the series, but in the end they were no match for the Michael Jordan-led Bulls. The Hawks were eliminated in five games.

The Atlanta Hawks franchise has become one of the top teams in the Eastern Conference. If the Hawks can add a few more pieces to their already solid lineup, the city of Atlanta will be soon be celebrating its first-ever NBA championship.

# Glossary

**American Basketball Association (ABA)**—A professional basketball league that rivaled the NBA from 1967 to 1976 until it merged with the NBA.

**assist**—A pass of the ball to the teammate scoring a field goal.

**Basketball Association of America (BAA)**—A professional basketball league that merged with the NBL to form the NBA.

**center**—A player who holds the middle position on the court.

**championship**—The final basketball game or series, to determine the best team.

**draft**—An event held where NBA teams choose amateur players to be on their team.

**expansion team**—A newly-formed team that joins an already established league.

**fast break**—A play that develops quickly down court after a defensive rebound.

**field goal**—When a player scores two or three points with one shot.

**Finals**—The championship series of the NBA playoffs.

**forward**—A player who is part of the front line of offense and defense.

**franchise**—A team that belongs to an organized league.

**free throw**—A privilege given a player to score one point by an unhindered throw for goal from within the free-throw circle and behind the free-throw line.

**guard**—Either of two players who initiate plays from the center of the court.

**jump ball**—To put the ball in play in the center restraining circle with a jump between two opponents at the beginning of the game, each extra period, or when two opposing players each have control of the ball.

**Most Valuable Player (MVP) Award**—An award given to the best player in the league, All-Star Game, or NBA Finals.

**National Basketball Association (NBA)**—A professional basketball league in the United States and Canada, consisting of the Eastern and Western conferences.

**National Basketball League (NBL)**—A professional basketball league that merged with the BAA to form the NBA.

**National Collegiate Athletic Association (NCAA)**—The ruling body which oversees all athletic competition at the college level.

**personal foul**—A player foul which involves contact with an opponent while the ball is alive or after the ball is in the possession of a player for a throw-in.

**playoffs**—Games played by the best teams after the regular season to determine a champion.

**postseason**—All the games after the regular season ends; the playoffs.

**rebound**—To grab and control the ball after a missed shot.

**rookie**—A first-year player.

**Rookie of the Year Award**—An award given to the best first-year player in the league.

**Sixth Man Award**—An award given yearly by the NBA to the best non-starting player.

**trade**—To exchange a player or players with another team.

# Index